'Who would write, who had anything better to do' Byron

Nothing Better to Do

David Charleston

Jardine Press 1999

Acknowledgements

Some of these poems have appeared in the following magazines:
*joe soap's canoe, Prop, Scheherazade, Scratch, Seam,
Smiths Knoll, The Wide Skirt.*

'On the March, 25 October 1992' appeared in the *Guardian*.

ISBN 0 9525594 7 1
© David Charleston 1999
Cover by James Dodds
Jardine Press
The Roundhouse
Lower Raydon
Suffolk

Mandy

Contents

I

II

I

On My Way to Work

Some days on my way to work
and I don't have to go this way
although I do have to go to work

I pass a man in his garden making baskets;
I always wave although
I have never met the man before.

Today I asked myself:
am I waving at him or
some forgotten part of me?

I don't know.
I wouldn't swap places
but I like to keep in touch.

The Professor and the Rain

For years it was like he was working in a foreign country,
speaking a foreign language;
he would send strange messages,
in blue trained chicks the algebraic sum
of the excitatory and inhibitory responses
to the red stimulus is +14 mm,
discarded proofs for his grand-daughter
to draw on the back of.

We would visit him for birthdays
take photographs of each other
drink wine and exchange gifts
eat, sleep and leave the next day
doused in kippers.

One morning, he needed help with the horses.
We were out in the barn, loading hay
into the back of an old Toyota
when the subject of sleep came up
and how, when it rained,
he would run out into this barn
just to get under the roof
and listen to the sound of it.

And then there was today:
we were on a walk in the woods when
he lay down under a tree and slept
while you and I stood, looking at each other,
with water streaming down our faces.

Another Book Fair

Out at dawn
a magpie picks over the guts of a rabbit
I spoil its breakfast

I do another book fair
swear it's the last time I lug these boxes
in and out of the car

The public leaf through my remains
nobody scares them off
they take all day

I pick up a Pasternak
'happy people do not watch clocks;
it seems they only lie in pairs and sleep.'

Faces

I put the book down . . .
A leaf on the carpet catches my attention
Like the black spots of chewing gum
On the staircase going down from the car park

I remember the faces of people
As I carried the broken vacuum cleaner
Over my shoulder
Like a huge fish through the crowds

I wonder what will become of us
I feel the side of my face
It comes away, slack in my hand,
Like pastry.

Mimesis

The man with the cigarette
leaned over the bridge
as the swan struggled upstream

not swimming but pushing off
against the bottom
with one foot then the other

rolling from side to side
in water as shallow
as a baby's breath.

Years later, he remembers
her white wings and the muddiness
going away like smoke.

On the Verandah

based on extracts from Orwell's last note-book at Cranham Sanatorium

Woken by a bad dream I step out on the verandah
the air is colder than a doctor's hand.

The most persistent sound is the song of birds
not much noise of radios can be heard

like back in the hospital where trolleys rattled
and old men in bath chairs coughed like cattle.

Everything is done in a more leisurely way
I live alone in a so-called chalet.

Here on Easter Sunday upper-class voices ring
a constant bah-bahing of laughter abt nothing

a sort of heaviness & richness combined with ill-will
the encmies of anything intelligent or beautiful.

No wonder everyone hates us so.
At 50, everyone has the face he deserves.

Leaks

For Mandy

Everything leaks.
The engine leaks,
the petrol tank leaks,
the radiator leaks.
I'm sure that if I could see it
electricity would be leaking
from around the base of the lamp
on my desk as I write.
The gutters leak,
the chimney leaks,
the roof leaks
even the cherry tree leaks —
stuff that looks like treacle
and hardens like amber.
I'm certain the compost heap leaks
the best part oozing out
and feeding the nettles
under cover of darkness.
I know I leak
small quantities of blood
that pass in my urine
and alarm doctors whenever
I'm asked for a sample.
Everything leaks.
Fortunately.
For best of all
is the slow warm leak of love
I feel around my heart
when I see you after
the shortest separation.

Bowling in the Wet Grass

Bowling in the wet grass
the cricket ball smelt
like an old crab

and the red came off
in my hands
and on my trousers.

At the end of the over
I stalked to the boundary
like a butcher.

More Notes About a Hare

For Robert

Stopped and picked up a dead hare from the road
found I'd locked the boot
chose to lie it down on the passenger floor.

As I drove along it carved out a huge place
in the corner of my eye
lying there, as big as a border terrier.

By the end of the journey
a small red berry had dropped from its mouth
and from under its tail, a glistening black olive.

On the March, 25th October 1992

To get there, I had to go by bike and by train.
I got soaked on the bike but the train driver
hailed me and said, 'Comrade, let me
dry your jacket on the engine.'

In London, I went to the Embankment
where thousands queued under banners and placards.
We fed the police horses with barley sugars
and officers sang the Internationale.

Standing in the rain for three hours,
the black dye from my motorcycle gloves
ran over my hands and smudged my eyes
where I rubbed back tears of joy.

I never made it to Hyde Park, but the attendant
at Liverpool Street Station toilets remarked
how it looked like I'd been down the mines.
'I should be so lucky,' I replied.

Sugar

Charlie Absolom was a large, bearded all-rounder
who trained on haymaking and beer;
he could bowl a good medium pace,
hit in lively fashion and field actively.

A member of Lord Harris's team to Australia in 1878
he rescued England with 52 at Melbourne in his only test.

On forsaking cricket soon afterwards
he travelled extensively and became a purser,
dying in agony at the Port of Spain, Trinidad
when a crane discharged a cargo of sugar on him.

Strangely, he was one of the few cricketers
who had never worn a cap.

from THE WHO'S WHO OF TEST CRICKET by C. Martin-Jenkins

What Matters

For Rick

On the way to your funeral
along the choked streets of the city,
I notice the tenderness
with which a publican waters
his hanging baskets and window boxes,
how in the early sunshine,
before the pub opens,
he draws out his task
ignoring any other kind
of business.

I have flowers for you on the back seat
strange-scented, wrapped and robbed
of relationship —
let me give you this man instead,
his back turned on the traffic,
paying attention to what matters.

On This Earth With Our Lives

Sometimes I cycle to work.
I like the idea of cycling to work.
This morning I cycled to work.

Along the back roads I came to a house
with a woman sitting in the bay window,
eating toast.

As I passed, I could see she turned to look
for a split second
before returning to her breakfast.

That's it, I thought
that's about the size of the impression
we make on this earth with our lives.

Poem for Jess

On the night of your first day
a new moon branded
the pitch black sky.

On the second night
a mist grazed
the soft knee of the hills.

On the third day
you came home
and night and day rolled into one.

Thomas, Look Out

Thomas, you are four days old.
Look out, your mother's breasts
Have swollen to the size of small zeppelins
And threaten to come down on your head.

A Suffolk Cyclist Forsees His Death

Apologies to W.B. Yeats and Roger

I know that I shall meet my fate
Somewhere along these Suffolk lanes
Some bastard in a Ford Sierra
Will cut across the road again.

Along these lanes where stitchwort startled,
Toadflax flamed, ground ivy grew
Where barn owls ghosted out of darkness,
Badgers sauntered, foxes flew.

And I will try to climb the hedgerow,
And I will try just squeezing past
But of all the sights I've seen in Suffolk
A Ford Sierra'll be my last.

Allotment

Less tortured than most
he returned from Africa
to become the poet of the allotment.

Just down from the Happy Eater
beside the singing motorway
he found his place.

There and on the cricket field
he escaped this world,
he created his own space.

Madly hoeing between the words
he pared his poem
down to nothing.

Early Retirement

Deliberately taking his time
on his way back with the paper
the ex-bank manager stops on the bridge
to communicate with nature.

White-haired, slightly gammy in one leg
but very far from sere
he enjoys this time of morning most
with the traffic hurrying near.

Only he knows on Monday
how unspeakably good it feels
to cross the road with *Times* aloft
and stick another spoke in the chariot's wheels.

On the Green

Billy is smoking
a cigarette on the green
he thinks with his cupped hand
he cannot be seen.

Waiting for the school bus
alone on the green
his mind withdraws into happiness
on a wave of nicotine.

And while he thinks that no-one sees
some of us understand
that for a moment, the whole world's held,
in Billy's cupped hand.

Responsibilities

And later, the moon
came to remind me
of my responsibilities

peering in through
the dirty window
raising a smile.

Borrowing from nature
is a process
of mutual consent.

Literature is something
to keep quiet about
in a poem.

At best earth
only teaches you
silence

the flower roots deep
in the soil so as
not to shriek in the wind.

Dirtying my hands
I go quieter
all the while

words are solely of wind and water
earth presses her fat forefinger
firmly against her lips.

II

Fishing Trips

For my father

Sitting on my bike
with a smack of sun and the smell of 2 stroke
I remember the Seagull outboard
and those fishing trips we went on

Going out every day
catching plenty of fish
and coming back cold
with salt and scales on our fingers

And I don't worry about
all the things we never said to each other
all that Jack Nicholson nonsense

I only miss those times
when we were young enough
to be old friends.

The Holiday Poem

(1)

In the playground behind the pub garden
the sound of tap dancing children
like a bonfire.

Our own amuse themselves
improvising on the broken furniture
avoiding bits of glass.

We drink and stare into the distance
where we think we can see ourselves
coming into focus.

(2)

In the scrapyard (in the rain)
creatures, perfectly camouflaged
slide out from under vehicles

like crocodiles
only the silver wrench glinting
and giving them away.

At the back of a Vauxhall Astra (estate)
we manage to deliver a petrol tank
by Caesarean section.

(3)

In the churchyard, a large packet of Mates
keeps close company
with a bottle of Beck's.

Outside on the pavement
a man shifting a wardrobe comes to a standstill.
He reaches inside and brings out a can of beer.

Later in the pub another man
takes an age to get a drink for his friend.
'I thought you'd gone to fucking Dorset,' he says.

(4)

In the beach hut, the dosser arranges his bags,
throws some scraps for the birds,
makes sure his arse is poking out the top of his trousers.

On the beach, a man enjoys some *Paris Texas* time with his son
building castle after castle which the sea destroys
while the boy looks in the opposite direction

where a woman with three small children
manages to put up a tent
in spite of the wind.

(5)

In the garden I sit out late
surrounded by white chairs
like doctors from a sanatorium.

The holiday is over.
I can't quite bring myself
to go back inside

preferring to stay here
hoping to read some meaning
into the faulty braille of this damp rug.

(6)

In the car, the air is so thick with silence
you could spread it with a shovel
and feed it to the pigs

and then the children start up.
Only your tribute to Munch
makes any impression.

I grip the road, feed it gently through my hands:
these are our lives and
I'm taking them home.

Askari

Each night I guard the white man
keep safe his inside
allow no one to enter

while I keep the outside
the infinite universe
to myself.

How much more fortunate
then am I
to entertain so many stars

while he complains at his wife
and teaches his children
to bolt doors and escape?

And yet he pays me
to keep the outside,
he who works under a single lamp

while I consult the heavens
and know
this kingdom is mine.

Still

The night is completely still:
liquid black shadows
lie under the trees
the moon paddles gently
through so many degrees
nothing disturbs
the peace that descends —
guarded by dogs
and security men.

Magadi

Time will pass
and we will forget
the moonscape of Magadi
and its soda lake

its crusty shores
and bubbling springs
how our eyelids fluttered
with flamingo wings.

Melville in Miami

Before we get on the plane,
my small son and I
squeeze soapy hands under the drier
in the Gents at Heathrow
like Ishmael and his ship-mates
squeezing sperm
on board the Pequod.

In the mall in Miami
I am gripped by a shopping frenzy:
buy 24 'cheerful coathangers' for $2.99
although I don't need them
and couldn't get any happier.
I see Melville's 'long rows of angels'
standing in line at the check-out.

Teaching in Florida

I am lucky —
at the bottom of the wall
on the left hand side of my classroom
I have a window 2 by 4.

On sunny days
(and there are many of these)
light streams in
and floods the corner.

When I show a video
I turn the lights off and enjoy
the shadow puppet effect
of the student sitting there.

The bad boys are drawn to it
would like to kick out the window
kick out the light
as they've done in other rooms.

I humour them, smile, say
'I wouldn't do that' but know
if they did I'd be out with them
into the light.

Life on the Condo

At night, males go out alone
to smoke, walk the dog or
neat reversal of the primitive
carry full sacks from their apartments
which they heave into the dumpster.

I notice the moon over Miami,
its ungiddy path across the lake;
it's only December 6th
there are lights everywhere,
lights on lights.

Inside my wife and children are sleeping
they already bear the scars
of too much freedom:
they all go home in their dreams.

I return to the dark kitchen
fumble for a fresh sack under the drainer
peel it white on the soft belly of the swing-top
like moonlight.

Key West

Unlike Ernest Hemingway
I'd just trimmed my son's fingernails
before putting him to bed

so when, in the customary darkness
of our good-night story-telling,
his hand overshot his face

he only managed to poke me
in the eye, not slice the cornea
and blind me for three months.

It hurt enough though and
weeps a little as I sit
sweltering on the veranda

as hot as Algeria
where Camus said he would give
'a hundred Hemingways for a Stendhal'.

There are probably
at least that many
roaming the bars tonight.

The Ballad of South Dade High

Dead dogs & Christmas trees lie along Krome
the sun struggles into the sky
farmers spray their crops with anti-freeze
I teach down at South Dade High.

This is a 'drug-free school'
and I'm in 'the noblest profession'
just pass me another doughnut
before we get on with the lesson.

Cages round the Coke machines
bars across the doors
the roof came down on the salad bar
the gym doesn't have a floor.

Tar fumes in the library
water through the ceiling
it helps build strength of character
so forget that sickly feeling.

The students are mostly kind to me
they understand the score
we're working on essential skills,
we're learning 'Less is More'.

Anyway, this is America
don't try to preach to me
you've got your Princess Diana,
we've got our Liberty.

So let's not get too heavy, sir
CHILL don't be so drastic
as De Lillo says in Libra *'Here*
the stars are fucking fantastic.'

Dead dogs & Christmas trees lie along Krome
the sun struggles into the sky
farmers spray their crops with anti-freeze
I teach down at South Dade High.

A New Beginning

from an advertisement in the Miami Herald

Advanced Tumescent Liposuction
Breast Enlargement & Reduction

Skin Peels & Skin Care
Removal of Unwanted Hair

Face & Eyelid Surgery
Nose Jobs a Formality

Permanent Make-up Free Consultation
Unique Penis Augmentation

Jowls Lifted Tummy Tucks
Butts as Firm as Pick-up Trucks

Tennis Elbow Brewer's Droop
How Far Can a Body Stoop?

Postures Fixed Spines Corrected
Major Credit Cards Accepted.

Notes on Leaving Miami

Fat woman in shorts wedged in corner of pool
enjoys a cigarette, inflates by the lungful

bags under her eyes as big as bathing rings
finishes her smoke, no need for water wings

launches across the shimmering blue
children capsize in ones and twos

and while we find it hard to look
David Hockney turns to Beryl Cook.

Curiously exotic or beyond the pale?
Farewell Miami and another white whale.